COMPOSITION:
GRAHAM

M. D. Nowak

WESTBOW
PRESS®
A DIVISION OF THOMAS NELSON
& ZONDERVAN

WestBow Press books may be ordered through booksellers or by contacting:

WestBow Press
A Division of Thomas Nelson & Zondervan
1663 Liberty Drive
Bloomington, IN 47403
www.westbowpress.com
844-714-3454

ISBN: 978-1-6642-5524-1 (sc)
ISBN: 978-1-6642-5525-8 (e)

Print information available on the last page.

WestBow Press rev. date: 01/31/2022

Thursday, August 31

This is my last day before I leave for school. Dad gave me this notebook to write down all the "big ideas" I'm gonna have. But I think I'll just use it as a journal/sketchbook.

I'm not sure how I feel about starting my first year of college. I'm sure most kids have mixed emotions.

But most kids aren't *fifteen*, like me.

ME   AVERAGE COLLEGE KID

I should be grateful to get this kick start for my future—and I am—but it's all so daunting and confusing.

Skipping ahead a couple of grades was bad enough, but now college? I'm going to be having classes with literal *adults*.

But hey, maybe it'll be good for me. Maybe I'll become more independent. I'm really gonna miss my family, though. And I'm nervous about meeting my new roommate.

I've never, ever had to share a room before. I asked my sister Danielle what it was like to be in the same room as my youngest sister, Nicole, and she just stared off into the distance dramatically.

(I'm sure she was just kidding. At least, I hope.)

←DANIELLE

But yeah, sharing a room is just one of the many things I'll have to get used to. And it's not even my biggest worry!

I'd better finish packing. More later.

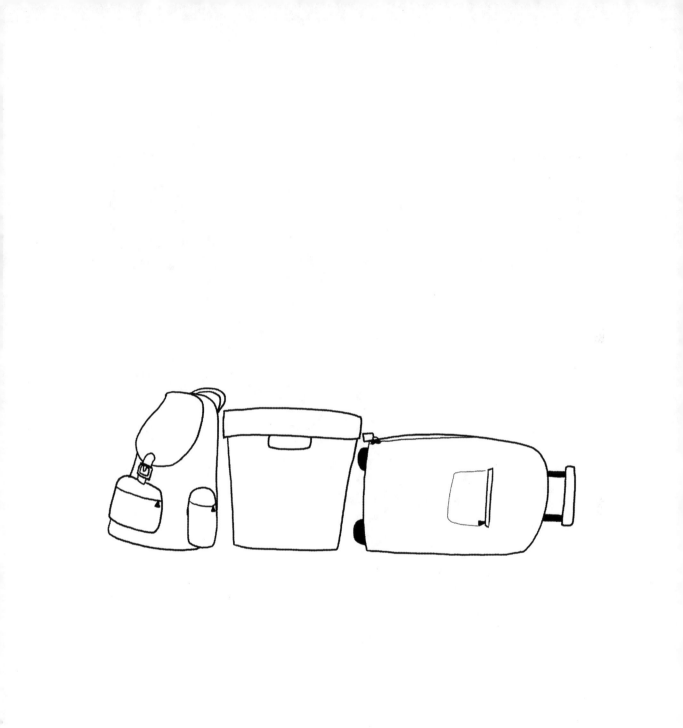

Friday, September 1

I'm writing this while on the bus. This morning I woke up early to take one last walk around the neighborhood. Josh (my dog) and I went around the block, like, three times before I felt ready to go home.

When I got back, Mom had a special breakfast for us, and Dad helped me load up my stuff in his car. I hugged everyone, tried not to notice Mom's sniffles, and jumped in the car with Dad. It was a ten-minute drive to the bus station, and Dad was giving me instructions the whole way.

"Call us when you get there, okay?"

"Yeah, Dad."

"You have money for lunch?"

"Sure, Dad."

"Did you remember your credit card?"

"*Yes, Dad!*"

When he dropped me off, Dad hugged me and said, "I'm proud of you, son."

That's when I almost started to cry. I don't think it had dawned on me until that moment that I was really doing it—going to college.

The university is only an hour away, and it's the school Mom and Dad went to, but I'm still scared! *Why?*
I'm familiar with the campus, so I shouldn't be nervous about getting lost. Mom said she'd visit next weekend after visiting her sister (who lives fifteen minutes from campus). I have no reason to worry. I'll be fine.

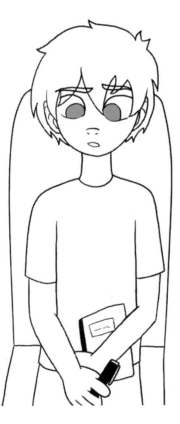

I'll be fine.

Saturday, September 2

Yesterday, after I got to school, I hauled my stuff to the dormitories, where a school rep met me and gave me my room key. He showed me to my dorm, where my roommate was already unpacked and waiting.

I started unpacking my things while he stood shyly to the side.
He cleared his throat and introduced himself. "Hey. I'm Max."
"Nice to meet you. I'm Graham."
"Uh ... yeah. Nice to meet you too."

I sort of laughed then. It's how I respond to awkward situations. Luckily, Max laughed too.

"So what major are you, Graham?"
"Undecided. I'm just gonna get my generals out of the way first. You?"
"English."
"Cool! So you like to read a lot?"

Max pointed to his desk. There was a *huge* box of books on it.

"I'm also on the cross-country team," he said.
"Are you a freshman as well?" I asked. I had assumed I'd be paired with another first-year, but I wanted to make sure.
Max nodded. "Yup. I'm a bit young for my grade, but yeah."

"Oh? How old are you?" I asked (with maybe a bit too much enthusiasm).
"I'm seventeen. My birthday is in two weeks, though."

Yes! I thought. *Another minor.* For the next two weeks, at least.

"I'm fifteen," I said, just to get that out of the way.
"Skip a couple of grades?"
"Yeah."
"Cool."
And that was that. I appreciated Max's attitude. Usually, I'm bombarded with questions like "Are you some kinda genius or something?"

Which, of course, makes me uncomfortable.
Yeah, I guess I'm smart, but it's not a big deal. School just came easily to me. That's all.

"Well, I hope you get settled all right," Max said. "I have a team practice. But I'll be back later."
"Okay," I said. "Later!"

And then I was alone. I didn't have orientation until four o'clock, which left me three whole hours.
For a while, I just stood in the middle of our room. Then I decided to give myself a tour. Our room had a small sink, a tiny bathroom, a minuscule closet, and a main room with a petite couch, two dressers, two desks, and a bunk bed.

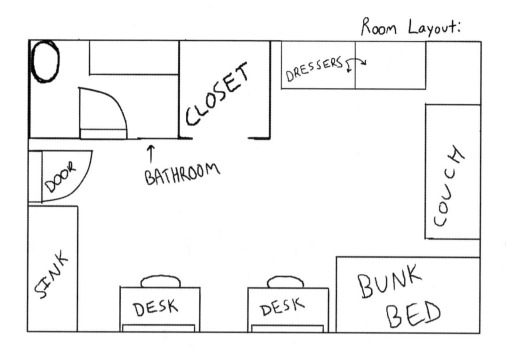

It looked like Max had claimed the bottom bunk, so I hoisted my stuff on the top bed. After an hour of struggling, I *finally* got my sheets on. Then I arranged my books and binders on my desk. After that, I organized and put away my clothes.

I still had an hour to kill, so I sat down to read. I'm currently into dystopian novels. *The Giver* is my favorite book. This will be my tenth time reading it.

Hmm. I wonder if Max likes *The Giver.* Wouldn't hurt to check his book box.

He has it. He's my new best friend.

Sunday, September 3

Orientation yesterday was long and boring. I felt so overwhelmed! Mostly, I kept to myself. I met a few people, but I only talked with them briefly, and I didn't even learn half of their names.

Since today is Sunday, there's no orientation or class-prep activities. Max went to church this morning, but I opted to stay in the dorm. I was already stressed; I couldn't go to another new place full of strange people.
Once Max was gone, I popped some popcorn, sat at my desk, and watched the live stream of my home church's service. I was halfway through when ...

I've never cried that hard before! Seriously!

I think my popcorn started getting waterlogged. I was hiccup-sobbing for a good fifteen minutes. Then I finally got a hold of myself.

— sigh

Was I homesick? Or just tired?

Calling my family with a strained, tear-roughed voice seemed like a bad idea (and FaceTime was definitely out of the question), so I took a nap.

I woke up when Max came back. He and I talked for a while. I told him I'd looked through his books (sorry!) and noticed he had a lot of my favorites.
He admitted that his family had told him he couldn't bring them all, but he'd stuffed the box in his car anyway.

As we talked, he must've noticed I was stressed or something, 'cause he asked if I wanted to go for a "light, calming jog" with him.

I had nothing better to do, and it beat sitting around dreading class tomorrow, so I said yes.

One thing I wanna know: who in the world jogs to get calm? Max was basically sprinting the entire time! While Mr. Athlete expertly navigated the streets, I was wheezing behind.

I do have to admit, though, after we got back (and I could breathe again), I did feel a lot better.

I was able to call my family, and I talked to them for a long time.

If I can just make it through this first week of classes, I think I'll be fine!

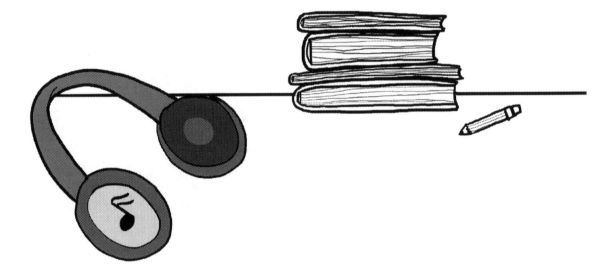

Monday, September 4

College is *so* different from high school!

For one thing, I only have two classes per day! Two! They each last about an hour. My Tuesday/Thursday classes go for about an hour and forty minutes.

Even with fewer classes, I *still* almost fell asleep in both my classes today.

Western Civ. is a lecture-style class, and it was going great until my eyes got heavy.

It was *super* hard to pay attention. So between classes, I got some coffee. I'm normally not a caffeine person, but I was desperate.

The coffee didn't help in the least! I still had trouble staying awake in my composition class—and I love writing (obviously)!

However, once I got back to the dorm, I couldn't take a nap because *that* was when the coffee decided to kick in.

I finished all my assignments in under an hour and just ... stood there, twitching.

When Max came in, he just stared at me for a moment. "Tough first day?" he asked.
"Y-yeah," I answered.
"Wanna run?"
"Yes."

So we went out for a three-mile run. I drained the caffeine from my system and felt *much* better.
I think I've learned my lesson. Tonight, I'll go to bed early, and I'll be sure to drink a noncaffeinated and nonsugary beverage tomorrow.

Tuesday, September 5

Today was a lot better, except for one thing:
the infuriating fire alarm!

I was sitting in my room, minding my own business, when a high-pitched *beep,
beep, beeeeeeep!* interrupted my studying.

It was 10:00 p.m.

Max and I rushed outside with the rest of the students. I failed to grab a jacket,
and of course, it was insanely cold outside!
I was in my pajamas, surrounded by other students who had blankets, slippers,
jackets, and other warm clothing.

I was feeling pretty lousy when all of a sudden this girl showed up.

To which I replied ...

She was so nice! Not a lot of older girls have talked to me at school. They usually don't know how to approach me. I either get:

But not *this* girl! She introduced herself as Delaney. I asked the basic questions— "What year are you?" (junior) and "What's your major?" (fashion design). Max, Delaney, and I talked until the fire department let us back in the building. Apparently, someone had just burned their dinner or something.

All in all, not a bad day!

Wednesday, September 6

I tried all day to find Delaney and give her back her blanket. In the end, I gave up and shoved it in my backpack.

To get some serious studying done, I headed to the library. It's just off of campus, so it's technically a public library, but a lot of students go there to study or hang out. I found a quiet corner and tried to concentrate.

Homework:

- History of Western Civ: Read Ch. 3 and answer Q's
- Composition: Start thinking of topic for paper
- Public Speaking: Make a speech flow chart
- Bio: Read Ch. 4 and article

All was going well until I hit a mental block. It happens to me now and then. I'll be going on homework, and suddenly my brain will quit.

So I did the only logical thing: I took a break!

To recharge, I need three things:

1. A snack
2. YouTube
3. Water

In that order.

I went to the vending machine and got some veggie straws, sat down in a new area, put in my earbuds, and watched some YouTube videos.

I mostly like to watch speed-paints. I love art. It's my go-to activity (as you may have guessed from my many doodles).

If I'm totally honest, I wish I could make a career of it—but I can't.

First off, I'm only halfway decent at it. Second, I feel like I'd let everyone down. I mean, can you imagine?

"Genius Boy Throws Away Potential"

So anyway, I was ~~being irresponsible~~ having fun and was following a speed-paint when—

It was *her.* Delaney.

I was doodling in the margins of one of my school notebooks when she just appeared behind me.

I dropped my pencil. "Oh, uh, hi! Um, thanks! I was just following a YouTube video." I turned my laptop screen toward her.

"Oh, cool! I love these," Delaney said enthusiastically.

Right. Fashion designer—artist.

I bashfully looked at my notebook and thought, *She thinks my drawing is good?*

Then I remembered myself. "Hey! I forgot to give you back your blanket. Sorry. And thanks again for letting me use it!"

"No prob," she replied. "Rule number one about living in the dorms: always have a jacket ready in case of fire alarms."

I stared at her blankly.

"Okay, maybe not rule number one," she amended. "But it's definitely important!"

"Heh. Yeah."

I hate awkward silences. I never know what to do. Also, what was I supposed to say? I'm not exactly stellar when it comes to talking to girls.

Delaney saved me by changing the subject. "So you like to draw?"

I smiled, relieved. "Yeah. It's a hobby."

She returned the smile. "You ever consider joining the Art Club on campus?"

"I wasn't aware there was one!" I responded.

I thought an art club might be fun. I could meet new people, make more friends. But I wouldn't feel comfortable unless I already knew someone in the club.

"Are you in Art Club?" I asked hesitantly.

"Oh, totally!" she answered. "We meet on Friday nights at 8:00 p.m. in the ceramics studio." She quickly scribbled down the room number in my notebook.

"That sounds like fun," I said.

"It is! I can't wait to see you there."

"Yeah. Yeah, I'll come, for sure!"

"Great! See ya around." She chipperly skipped away.

A club.

I got invited to a club!

Thursday, September 7

Max was gone today for a meet. Though it was kinda lonely in the dorm, it was nice to have some "me time." After class (and after homework) I plopped on my bed, pulled out my phone, and watched some baseball!

Baseball is my favorite sport. My dad and I are obsessed with it. I told him that he's not allowed to talk with me until I watch all the games I've missed. Dad is notorious for accidentally spoiling game scores, movie endings, and the like.

Besides spending time with Dad, I also love watching a good ball game 'cause it's the only time I can let my emotions out.

Here's me normally:

- Even-keeled
- Emotionless
- Expressionless
- Amiable

Here's me when I'm watching baseball:

- Excitable
- Loud
- Up-and-Down
- Obnoxious

Yeah, it's a problem.
But I had a good time.

Friday, September 8

Finally, the day came! Art Club!

I was excited (and nervous) through all my classes. When I finally got back to my room, I quickly gathered some art supplies—this notebook, pencils, some markers—and hurried over to the ceramics room.

When I arrived, I was surprised to find a variety of people. There were artists (duh!), athletes, and some awkward newbies (like me). Max was even there!

Athlete   Noob   Artist

The meeting started with the club president introducing herself: Mellie. She ran over the agenda quickly—funding, openings for positions, etc. Then she said that this first meeting would be a "get-to-know-you" open time. Basically, you could walk around and meet new people or just sit and draw—totally up to you and at your leisure.

I said hi to Max and Delaney, of course, and then I sat down at an empty table. I'm better at observation than I am at conversation.

Mellie made eye contact with me from across the room and started toward me.

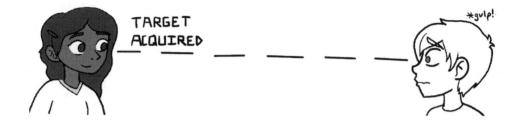

"Hi!" she said. "What's your name?"

"I'm Graham," I replied.

"Nice to meet you, Graham! Are you a freshman?"

"Yes," I responded (notice my speaking prowess).

"Well then, welcome to the school! Do you need help with anything? Advice?"

"Um, no," I said slowly, thinking. "Well, actually, yes. I'm just wondering how you found your major. I assume you're in the art and design department?"

"You betcha!" she exclaimed. "I'm an animation major. I've always loved cartoons, so I figured it was the perfect place for me."

"What's that like?" I asked. "I mean, making a career out of something that most people just consider to be a hobby."

"Well, it was hard at first," she said, brow furrowing. "My parents were concerned that I was going into a field that would be difficult to make a living in. But you know," she said with a conspiratorial smirk, "you can actually make a decent amount of money being an artist nowadays. I'm not in it for the money anyway. The key to picking your major is finding that thing you love, the thing you'd do voluntarily without the promise of payment."

"That sounds nice and all," I said, "but what about potential and career aptitude? Shouldn't you do what you're good at? Like, what if someone wanted to be an artist, but they were more skilled and suited for, say, being a lawyer?"

"It is up ... to ... you," she answered.

Well, *thanks*.

We talked some more, discussing our favorite types of art and our favorite cartoons. Mellie was very nice. She had to go talk to everyone else, so she said goodbye and wandered over to another group of people.

My friend count went up by one.

I decided to follow Mellie's example and be more friendly and outgoing. I quickly moved from table to table, introducing myself, offering a quick handshake, and trying my best to remember names.

By the end of the meeting, I had met eleven new people, drawn three things (someone had lent me good paper and pencils to draw with), and promised Mellie that I'd come back next week.

I think I've found where I belong.

Saturday, September 9

As promised, Mom came down to visit today after seeing my aunt Dee (who, unfortunately, couldn't make it—but she sent some cookies along with Mom to give to me!).

Mom met me in the parking lot outside my door and gave me a huge hug.

"Hi, sweetie!" she exclaimed. "Oh, I've missed you so much! How are you?"
"Fine, Mom," I answered.
"So where do you want to go? A restaurant? Do you need groceries?"
"Well, I need to get more toilet paper. Then we could go eat. I'm already sick of cafeteria food," I said.
"Great! Is your roommate coming?"
"Nah. He has a meet today."

"Oh, that's right, he's a runner," Mom laughed. "I can't believe he got you into that."

"I know! I used to hate running when we had to do drills in baseball. But it's not so bad. It can be a good stress relief."

Mom smiled. "Well, I'm glad you've got friends and fun activities. How are your classes?"

I grimaced. "They're fine, but I can't wait till I can take more than just generals."

"Do you have an idea of what you want your major to be?"

I winced.

Mom opened the car door. "It's okay if you don't know yet. You've got a bit of time."

I slumped into the passenger seat. If only I could tell her, with confidence, that I wanted to be an artist.

But I couldn't. 'Cause I really don't know if I do.

We made a quick stop at a Walmart. Since coming to college, I have learned the hard way that you *always* need to check to see if you're running low on the TP.

Anyway, we went to my favorite fast-food place, A+W, next. I don't know why I love it so much. Probably for the root beer.

ELEMENTS OF A
Perfect
ROOTBEER FLOAT:
★ Ice cream + rootbeer are pre-mixed
★ Chilled glass

It was a good time. I asked Mom how the rest of the family was.

- Danielle has a soccer match coming up on Tuesday.
- Nicole is starting to learn to play the saxophone.
- Dad is on a fishing trip till Monday.

"And I'm here with you," Mom concluded, tousling my hair.

We finished eating and shopping, then Mom drove me back to the dorms. She parked the car and turned to face me.

"Sweetie, I hate to ask you to do this, but could you start looking for a job? Maybe on campus? Your scholarships and financial aid are helping, but money is still tight, you know?"

"I understand," I replied. "I'll see what I can do."

"Great. I love you, honey!" She gave me a peck on the cheek.

"Love ya, Mom," I said, bolting from the car.

(I hope no one saw that!)

I spent the rest of the day alone, cleaning my room, finishing homework, and listening to music. And drawing.

Tomorrow, I'll go to church, and then ...

Job search.

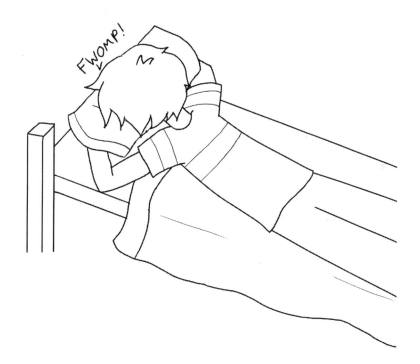

Oh, boy.

Sunday, September 10

Why does Max go to an *early* service?

I shouldn't complain. I'm lucky to have a fellow Christian as a roommate.

We went to his home church since Max is from around the area. It was nice.

While we were listening to the sermon, I was doodling in the service program. I swear I was paying attention. Sometimes drawing helps me focus when I'm listening to something. It's also a good way to remember what I've learned. I'm a visual learner, so if I need to recall something, I usually associate it with an image.

Max must've noticed my art, 'cause on the drive home he asked me about it.

"Ah, well, I dunno," I replied.
"Why not? I've seen you draw. You're good! And you're always doing it."
"That doesn't mean I'm going to make a career of it," I said.

"I ask again, why not?"

"Well, uh," I stuttered, "what about you? You were at Art Club. Why don't *you* become an artist?"

Max gave me a side glance. "I already am. But I create art through words."

"Oh. I guess you're right," I conceded.

He pulled into the drive-through at McDonald's. "It's okay to have big dreams," he said. "I see you working so hard at your classes, and that's great, but the first time I saw you laugh—really laugh—and let loose was at that Art Club meeting."

"Really?" I'd never realized that I seemed so uptight to those around me.

"Yup," Max said. He pulled forward and rolled down his window. "I'll have two small vanilla shakes, please."

I quickly pulled out my wallet and searched for a five-dollar bill.

"No need, man," Max said, giving the worker his credit card. He paid for the shakes and picked them up at the next window.

"Thanks!" I said.

"No prob," he responded. He handed me a shake and a straw. "This is kind of a tradition for my family—a little something sweet to hold us over till lunch."

"Well, I like this tradition," I said, picking off the cherry and inserting the straw.

Max swiped the cherry from me and popped it in his mouth. "I'll consider this my thanks," he teased.

I'm really lucky to have such a good friend.

Monday, September 11

Today ... wasn't the best.

My alarm didn't go off for some reason, so I was late to class. It was Western Civ too.

I was only tardy by ten minutes, but that was enough for the professor to give me an earful about "responsibility" and "becoming an adult."

I don't need to be told those things! Yeah, I'm sure he was just trying to look out for my future, and I didn't mean to show him any disrespect by being late, but—

My day went from bad to worse when I realized that in my haste, I had forgotten my student ID, which meant I couldn't buy lunch.

I was on campus all day and had to go to a job interview. Since Mom told me I need a source of income, I decided to check the campus website yesterday because they post student employment positions there.

So yesterday, I logged on and narrowed down the options based on my interests and qualifications (and, of course, how much I'd be paid). My top three choices were:

- Janitor ($10/hour)
- Usher ($9.50/hour)
- Ticket Office ($10.25/hour)

I thought having a job as an usher would be cool, so I filled out that application first. The job description said that I'd work every time a show or concert was being performed in the auditorium/theater.

Well, I showed up to the interview and pretty much got the job on the spot.

The events director explained that they need as many ushers as possible since workers sometimes have scheduling conflicts (which makes sense, since most shows/concerts happen on weekends).

He also told me that the job will require me to dress in a white shirt, black pants, and black dress shoes. They'll provide me with a name tag and the classic usher's black vest.

I hope this job will help Mom and Dad. I won't be able to work all the time, but at least it'll be something!

Anyway, back to the bad parts of my day ('cause getting the job was the only good part).

As I mentioned, I hadn't eaten anything all day. I stumbled back to the dorm, tired and hungry. I was just about to grab my ID to get something to eat when ...

The fire alarm went off again!

We waited outside for *an hour* before they let us back in. By now, my stomach was hurting pretty bad.

I just need food, I told myself. I made my way to a vending machine and inserted a dollar bill.

At this point, I just pushed a random button. I didn't care what I got to eat; I just needed food *immediately!*

Of course, it took me ten tries till the bill actually went in. But then—

The power went out.

Dejectedly, I made my way toward the stairs. Next thing I knew, I was lying on the ground, with someone shaking my shoulder.

I got up, wobbling. "I-I think so," I said.

Man, I can't believe I passed out!

"Here, let me help you," the guy said. He let me lean on his shoulder.

"Thank you."

"What floor?"

"Second," I replied.

Together, we hobbled up the stairs.

"Do I need to get anyone?" he asked.

"Uh, no, thanks ..." I looked at him questioningly.

"Luis," he said.

"No, thanks, Luis," I said. "I think I'm just tired and hungry."

"Ah, yeah. Take care of yourself, buddy!" Luis reached into his backpack and pulled out a granola bar. He handed it to me.

"Thanks!" I exclaimed, ripping off the wrapper and digging in.

"No prob," he said with a shrug.

We kept walking until I pointed out my room. I thanked him once again and assured him I wasn't about to keel over.

"Okay, bro. But just know that my room is just down the hall. Knock anytime!"

"I will," I said.

I went into my room and immediately crashed on my bed, putting an end to a (mostly) miserable day.

But I suppose I can't really complain. After all, I got a new job and a new friend!

Tuesday, September 12

When I woke up this morning, I found a present on my desk.

Here's what the note said:

Graham,

> I know yesterday was hard on you. Just take care of yourself, okay? I'm here for you.
>
> — Max

I ate the muffin on my way to class and decided that I had to do something special for Max.

His birthday is this Saturday. I wondered what I could do to celebrate with him. I'll definitely get him something for a present, but I decided that maybe I should plan a party as well.

I would have to find some of his friends and invite them, and that was gonna be the hard part. I'm actually pretty shy.

But I knew Delaney and figured she probably would want to come. I could also see who is on the cross-country team and invite them.
I quickly texted Delaney (she had put her contact info in my phone when I wasn't looking during Art Club). She responded within seconds.

She asked me about the details, and I told her I was thinking of having the party Saturday night. She also asked if I'd like her to buy a cake for Max.

Seriously, she's the nicest person ever!
I told her, "That'd be great!"

So now we have at least one guest *and* a birthday cake!

I still needed to somehow contact the cross-country runners. Luckily, we have sports rosters on our school's website. I looked up the guys' and girls' running teams and sent a group email to them through the campus directory.

To: (12 recipients)

Subject: Max's Surprise Party!

Hello, all!
I am Graham, Max's roommate.
His birthday is on Saturday and I wanted to invite you all to his surprise party! Please feel free to invite anyone else you think he'd want to come.
The party will be in our dorm—

I gave the details, crossed my fingers, and hit send!

I really hope everything works out.

Wednesday, September 13

I had a pretty chill day today. I had decided to relax and listen to some music when Danielle called.

I was really excited to talk with her. Danielle is only three years younger than me, so we've always been pretty close.

Right now, she's in training for an elite soccer league. She was on her middle school's team, but the league can provide her with more opportunities.

Her dream is to one day make the US Women's Soccer Team, play in the World Cup, and get the Golden Cleat Award!

I answered the phone. "Hi, Dani! What's up?"

"Not much," she replied. "Just wanted to say hi."

"Cool. How's soccer going?"

"Swell," she said, chipperly. "It's hard work, but I love it! How's college?"

"Can't complain. I'm starting to meet more people and make new friends," I said.

"In fact," I added conspiratorially, "I'm throwing a party on Saturday."

"You are *not*!"

"Am too. It's Max's birthday. I wanted to surprise him."

"Well, that's nice," Dani said.

"I hope he likes it. Hey, since you're an athlete too, what do you think I should get him for a present?" I asked.

"Hmm," she said. I could imagine her tapping her chin in thought. "Does he have a good athletic bag?"

"Yeah, his seems pretty new," I answered.

"How about socks?" she asked excitedly.

"Socks?"

"Yeah! Athletes always need 'em! Oh, and you could get him a keychain. It's always nice to have one so you can spot your bag right away."

"Great! Thanks for the advice," I said.

"No problemo! I've gotta run, but let me know how the party goes. Love ya, bro."

"Love ya, sis."

And she hung up.

Okay, now I have a mission. Thanks to Danielle, I've got some ideas for the perfect gifts.

Thursday, September 14

As I was heading back from class today, I ran into Delaney. She was walking with some guy. I stopped to say hello and asked if she could still make it to Max's party on Saturday.

"Well, of course!" she replied.

"Great!" I said.

"By the way, Graham, this is my boyfriend, Eric," she said, introducing the guy next to her.

"Nice to meet you," I said. "Um ... I guess if you wanna come to the party as well, you're welcome to."

"Thanks," Eric replied. "I'll try to make it, but I might not have time. I have a big project to work on."

"Eric is a fashion design major, like me," Delaney explained. "Right now, he's working on developing his own design to print on fabrics."

"Woah, you can do that?" I asked.

"That's the plan," Eric said.

Suddenly, a light bulb went off in my head.

"Wow! Really?" I couldn't believe Eric and Delaney had the resources for something like that!

"Sure. Just make the designs digital."

"Oh. I don't know how," I said, dejected.

"I can show you!" Delaney offered. "If you have time right now, we could go to the computer lab."

"Okay. Let's do it!"

So Delaney, Eric, and I walked to the lab. Delaney showed me some art and design software and got a drawing tablet from the back of the room. It took a while to set up, but it worked properly once everything was plugged in.

"Now there's a bit of a learning curve to it," Delaney warned.

I nodded and opened up Photoshop. I began to draw, and Delaney and Eric gave me advice as I started developing my design.

"Thanks so much for your help," I said as I worked.

"No biggie," Delaney said with a shrug.

"So," I began, searching for conversation topics, "how did you two meet?"

"Oh, I've known Eric since we were kids," Delaney said. "We'd always been friends, but last year we decided to start going out."

"Yeah," Eric said, blushing. "It took me a while to work up the nerve."

"Did you follow each other to college?" I asked.

"Not really," Delaney said. "We went to the same high school, and we both wanted to design clothes, so our guidance counselor ended up recommending the same college for the both of us."

"I don't mind," Eric said, bumping Delaney's shoulder.

I smiled and continued drawing. "What made you guys decide on fashion design?"

"I always liked the idea of designing my own clothes," Delaney explained. "Plus, I love sewing."

"And I want to design costumes for films," Eric said. "Especially superhero movies!"

"That's cool!" I replied. It sounded like a fun major.

With one more tap of the tablet pen, I finished my design.

"Awesome!" Eric exclaimed.

"And, uh, here are the socks I want to put the design on," I said, handing them over. "I bought them last night and forgot to take them out of my backpack."

"Well, lucky for us you did!" Delaney said, taking them from me.

"The lab has the supplies to make keychains, so don't worry about buying any of that stuff," Eric said. "I'll work on that and the socks, and I'll give the finished products to Delaney to give to you in case I can't make it."

"Great!" I said. "I really can't thank you enough."
"Like I said, not a big deal." Eric patted me on the shoulder. "It's always nice to help a fellow artist." He waved goodbye and headed out the door.

Delaney was just about to follow him when she turned around and started rummaging through her backpack.

"Graham," she said. "I just got a new drawing tablet, so I don't need my old one. It's a bit dated and low-tech, but would you like it?"
"Oh, I couldn't," I said.
"Sure, you can. Here," she said, tearing a piece of paper from a notebook. "This is the name of a free drawing program to download. It's a lot like Photoshop. I think you'd enjoy it."

"Well, at least let me pay you for the tablet," I said.
"Nah, it's not worth much," she insisted.
"Well ... thanks," I said as she placed it in front of me.
"My pleasure," she said with a smile. "Well, see ya later! Good luck!"

I really don't know how I ended up with such great friends.

Friday, September 15

Delaney just gave me the drawing tablet yesterday, and I've already spent over six hours using it!

draw
draw

I think I might've annoyed Max a bit.

But I couldn't help it! Drawing is so fun! I even found a website where I can upload my designs and order them to be made on T-shirts. How cool!

Anyway, after my drawing spree, I decided that I should get some *actual* homework done. I headed to the dorm's end lounge to study since Max had fallen asleep, and I didn't want to wake him.

I set my books down, opened up my laptop, and got to work. After a while, someone else came in and sat across from me. It was Luis!

"Hey, amigo, how you doing?" he asked.

"Hey, Luis. I'm good. You?"

"Can't complain," he said. "By the way, I never caught your name."

"Oh, duh!" I exclaimed. "I'm Graham. Man, sorry about that."

"Ah, that's okay. I don't expect a guy to remember to introduce himself after he keels over."

I laughed. "Thanks for understanding."

"So you've been doing okay, then?"

"Yeah," I replied. "I was just overworked and undernourished. I'm fine now."

"Good," Luis said. "You've gotta learn to take time to relax and have fun. I learned that the hard way my freshman year."

"Oh?" I asked.

"I fell asleep during a lecture," Luis explained. "The professor had to wake me up when the next class started coming in."

"Oof!" I exclaimed.

"I know, right?" he said, chuckling.

"Well, hey, if you need to relax this weekend, I'm throwing a birthday party for my roommate tomorrow. You're welcome to come."

"Who's your roommate?"

"His name is Max."

Luis thought for a moment. "Long legs, brown hair, kinda shy?"

"Yeah," I said. "You know him?"

"Totally," Luis replied. "He's in my English Lit class. I'd be happy to come!"

"Awesome," I said. "I'll put you on the guest list!"

"Sweet," he said. "Hey, whatcha got there?" He pointed to my tablet.

"Oh, uh, a drawing tablet. My friend gave it to me," I said.

"No way!" Luis exclaimed. "You're an artist?"

"I–it's a hobby."

"Can I see some of your work?" he asked.

I thought about saying no, but I didn't want to be rude. So I pulled up the drawings I had done that morning.

"Dude! These are awesome!" he said. "Hey, I know this is kinda random, but would you be willing to do some illustrations for me?"

"Uh, depends," I replied. "What are they for?"

"Well, I'm a journalism major," he explained, "and I have a writing project coming up where I have to make my own newspaper. It's fake—only for fun—but I need someone to do the comics for the funny pages."

"Um ..."

"I'll pay you for it," Luis promised. "Five dollars per comic strip. Maybe do three of them?"

"Uh ..." What did I have to lose? It sounded like a fun thing to do. "Sure, why not?" I responded.

"Aw, yeah! Thanks," he said, high-fiving me.

So I guess I'm a cartoonist now.

I'll have to come up with some ideas for characters and fun little stories.

IDEAS:

Baseball comic?

Dog comic?

Comic about college?

Saturday, September 16

Today was the big day! I was so excited, I could barely contain my smile (I tried to suppress the enthusiasm, though, so Max wouldn't suspect that anything was up).

I had the party scheduled for 6:00 p.m. Max did his evening run at five, so I had an hour to set up the room. I cleaned everything (i.e., shoved our stuff under the bed) and threw up some streamers. Then I ordered a pizza and set up my desk with drinks and snacks.

Within fifteen minutes, Delaney and Eric showed up.
"Hey, guys!" I said excitedly as I let them in.
"Hello, Graham," Delaney said. She was carrying a birthday cake. I directed her to the snack area. She put it down, then nudged Eric.
Eric handed me a shoebox with a flourish.
I opened it up and saw the socks and key chain.
"This is perfect. Thanks!" I exclaimed. "Now I can wrap it. It'll be from all of us!"
Eric smiled. "I'm glad I could make it."

"Knock, knock," someone said outside the door.
"Luis, hey!" I said.
He came in, carrying a plate of cookies. "My roommate likes to bake, so I thought I'd bring some chocolate chip cookies as a gift."
"Fantastic! Thanks," I said, putting them on the table. "Luis, this is Eric and Delaney."
"A pleasure," Luis said.

They all started talking while I wrapped the present and finished setting up. Pretty soon, some of Max's teammates started filtering in. Not all could make it, but we had a decent turnout.

Max came back to the room at 6:15 and immediately stepped back in shock.

"Graham? Wha-? You guys!" He excitedly joined our happy little group.
"Happy birthday!" everyone yelled.
"Oh, man! I don't know what to say. Thanks, everyone!"

With that, the party commenced. We talked, ate food, played some card games, and even put in a movie (*The Giver*, of course).
A few people had brought gifts, so we had Max open them up near the end.

Max got a T-shirt with a running logo, a new book, a set of colored pens, and the socks and keychain I made.

Everyone left around 10:00 p.m. Max helped me clean up (though he really didn't need to; it was *his* birthday party).
He kept saying how much he liked his gift.
"I'm glad you're glad," I said. "I wanted to do something special for you. You're a good friend."
"Well, you are too," he said.

We got the room back to spick-and-span, or at least as clean as you can get with two teenagers.

"Just ... thanks for being there for me," Max said as he got ready for bed.
"Ditto," I replied as I lay down.

Sunday, September 17

Max was gone today to be with his family, so I watched church online again. Afterwards, I didn't have any homework to do, so I got to work on the comics Luis asked me for.

My first idea was a baseball comic. I scrapped that one because it would cater only to sports fans.

My second idea was to do a comic about a dog. I eventually decided against it because it felt like I was ripping off Snoopy from *Peanuts*.

So that left me with my last idea: a comic about a college student. It seemed like a sound idea. Everyone reading the newspaper (namely, students) would be able to relate to it. And, as far as I know, there isn't a comic series about college students.

Plus, I have lots of source material!

So for now, I think I'll just write and draw about actual things that have happened to me.

College Comics   By Graham Russell

Monday, September 18

Today was my first day of work! The orchestra was having a concert, so I took a shift.

It was actually really fun! I took tickets and led people to their seats. Then I got to just relax and watch the show. When it was done, all I had to do was thank people as they exited and then help clean up.

Not the worst job in the least. I got four hours in (so about $40).

I've spent the rest of the night working on a paper. (It is 10:00 p.m. while I'm writing this. My paper still isn't done, but I need time to de-stress and think. Plus, it's not due till Friday.)

The paper is supposed to be about an exciting or trying moment in your life.

Welp, since I'm still going through a trying period right now, I decided to lean to the "exciting" side.

Here's what I have so far:

Driver's Ed

Driver's ed was an exciting time in my life. I'm sure all kids get pumped about learning to drive, but for me, even more so! It's rare that I get to be a "normal" kid. Driver's ed was an exception. I was in a small class with kids who were all my age. The teacher was very nice but serious. He taught us the basics of what we'd need to know on the road: what different signs meant, how to take care of a car, etc. My favorite lesson was about drunk driving. I don't plan on ever driving while intoxicated, but I enjoyed the exercise we did. To prove that you can't drive drunk, the teacher had us wear goggles that distorted our vision. Then we had to complete a test. The test was simple enough: walk in a straight line. But we all failed! The glasses made it so hard to see that I ended up slamming into the wall! As fun as the classroom lessons were, I was nervous for when we actually got behind the wheel. Driving seems like it would be easy—I mean, over half of the general population can drive—but it's not. The first time I went out with the instructor, I hit the gas instead of the brake and nearly ran into a tree! But over time, I was able to improve enough that I could drive well—or I should say, well enough that the instructor didn't have to yank the wheel from me!

That's as far as I've gotten.

Now that I'm thinking about it, I should really get back to practicing driving. I plan on taking my test in January, when I turn sixteen.

Maybe Max would let me drive his car.

No, never mind. Bad idea. I'll just practice whenever I'm home.

Tuesday, September 19

I gave my comics to Luis today.
His reaction:

These are perfect! Thanks, *amigo*.

"When are you turning your paper in?" I asked.
"My first edition is due Friday. Then I print out two more—one at mid-semester and one for my final."
"Cool!" I said. "You'll have to let me read it."

"Totally!" Luis reached into his pocket and pulled out some money. "Here's what I owe ya."
"No, no!" I said. "It was my pleasure. Really!"
"I can't just *take* your art, man," Luis replied. "Besides, real newspapers pay their artists, so I should too."
I hesitantly took the money. "Thanks."
"Don't mention it! I paid my photographer as well, so I'm not giving you any special treatment." He winked.
I laughed. "Well, next time I expect a raise."

He punched my shoulder.

I don't know why, but my confidence was really boosted by that.

The truth is, I didn't really care about the money.
That made me think of Mellie and how she'd said that picking a career shouldn't be based on financial gain.

Am I ... an artist?

Wednesday, September 20

I was up pretty much all night thinking about my revelation.

If I'm truly an artist—I mean, if it's truly what I want to be—then how should I go about it? What specific major do I choose? What classes do I take?

Someone, HELP me!

All the stress was getting to me, so after I coasted through class, I decided to call my family. Maybe talking over my options with them would give me clarity.

But when I called, no one answered. So I tried again. This time, Nicole picked up.
"Hi, Graham!" she yelled into the phone.
I winced. "Hi, sis," I said in a quieter tone, praying she'd get the hint.
She did. "How are you?" she said a bit more quietly.
"I'm fine. How are you?"
"Well, I'm bored," she whined. "Mommy and Daddy went out, so now it's just Dani and me. But she's outside playing soccer."
"Oh," I replied. "So what have you been up to?"
"Marie and I are playing saxophone!"

Marie is Nicole's rag doll, named after Marie Curie, the scientist. Nikki is a bit of an oddity for her age—she loves jazz and science. But she's also super energetic and fun! Everyone loves her.

"Have you and Marie been practicing a lot?" I asked.
"Mm-hmm!" she said. "You wanna hear?"
I tried frantically to stop her. "No, really, that's—"
Too late.

My eardrums were assaulted with a blasting rendition of "Twinkle, Twinkle Little Star."

She was pretty good, actually. It's just that saxophones are one of the *loudest* instruments!

But I applauded her after she was done. "That was very good, Nikki!" I said.
"Thanks! I've been practicing that song every single day."
"Wow! You must really love the saxophone."

"It's my favorite instrument!" she exclaimed.

"Do you ... want to be a musician even more than you want to be a scientist?" I asked.

"Um ... I dunno," she said. "I like music and science so much I can't decide between them."

"Huh."

Why was I looking to my six-year-old sister for advice about college? Well, "out of the mouths of babes comes wisdom," I guess.

"So anyway, it was nice to talk to you and hear you play!" I said.

"Yeah. I'll have Mommy and Daddy call you back. Bye, Graham! Marie says bye-bye too!"

"Bye, Nikki. Bye, Marie!" I said.

After hanging up, I flopped down on my bed. Everyone has things they love to do, right? But how do you decide what you should do as just a hobby versus what you should do for a career?

Nikki doesn't realize how good she has it right now.

Thursday, September 21

I woke up today with a massive headache.

Classes were torture, so I headed back to the dorm right away as soon as they were done.

When my head hurts, I can't eat, sleep, think, or do *anything*. When Max came in, he looked worse than I felt.

"I failed a test," he said.

"Aw, man, I'm sorry," I replied, cradling my head in my hands.

Max tossed me an ice pack from the freezer.

"Thanks," I said.

He came over to sit next to me on the couch. "I just don't get it," he said. "I've been studying really hard. Why can't I do anything right?"

"What class are you talking about?" I asked.

"English 250," he answered. "I guess I'm just a horrible test taker. My memory isn't the greatest."

To be honest, I had noticed that Max had difficulty remembering names and such. "You probably need a new study strategy. Have you tried flashcards?" I asked.

"Yeah. Doesn't work."

"Well, what kind of learner are you? Audio, visual, oral...?"

"Uh," Max said, "I don't know. Probably visual?"

"Me too!" I said. I winced. Getting excited hurt my head even more.

Max went to the cupboard and got out some Tylenol. He gave me two tablets, along with a glass of water.

"What do *you* do to study?" he asked.

I downed the medicine, thinking. "Well," I replied, "I try to envision the information by associating terms and definitions with pictures."

Max stared at me blankly.

How to explain? "Uh, how about I show you an example?" I suggested.

I quickly drew two characters on a piece of notebook paper.

"These guys are how I remember that protons are positive, and electrons are negative!"

"Oh, you make characters!" Max exclaimed. "Neat idea. I guess I can give that a try. Though I might think in terms of book characters I already know rather than making up new ones."

"Fair enough," I said.

"Thanks, man," Max said, standing up. He looked a bit happier.

I nodded, pressing the ice pack more firmly on my head.

Max looked at me with concern. "You gonna be okay?"

"Sure," I said. "I just haven't been getting a whole lot of sleep lately."

"Is it a medical issue? Or just stress?"

"Just stress," I said.

Max sat back down.

"It's just ..." I sighed. "I think I want to decide on a major."

"Cool!" Max said.

"Yeah, cool," I grumbled. "But what if my choice ends up being the wrong one?"

"So what? At least you'll have tried!" Max exclaimed.

I paused. "You think?"

"Yeah! You don't have to know for sure what your future will be. There's no way you could possibly plan for your whole life while you're still a teen!"

Wow. He had a point.

"Should I do it?" I wondered out loud. "Should I become an artist?"

Max looked me dead in the eye. "Dude, yes!" he said.

Then I guess I'm doing it.

Max whooped and slugged me in the arm. Then he apologized profusely when he saw that my head was about to explode.

"I guess it's just a matter of choosing an art and design major," I said.

"Ask around at Art Club tomorrow," Max suggested.

"Yeah. Yeah, that's what I'll do!" I decided.

With that, my fate was sealed.

Look out, artists! Here I come!

Friday, September 22

This morning, I texted my parents about my decision. Here's how they responded:

I should have known they'd be supportive of me! My parents have always been my number one fans, and I count myself lucky.

I remember at my first-ever baseball game, they wore face paint and had those foam finger things. And I was only seven!

I know they'll cheer me on in whatever I do.

However, I still want to be responsible and cause them as little worry as possible. So I did as Max suggested—I talked to other art students.

It was out of my comfort zone a bit, but it turned out okay!

This was my third week attending Art Club, so I was pretty relaxed around the usual crowd. All I had to do was find one student from each art and design major. Not too hard.

Here are all the art programs our school offers:

- Animation
- Graphic design
- Illustration
- Studio art
- Fashion design

You can also create your own major by talking to an advisor and picking specific courses to take.

I already know a bit about fashion design because of Delaney and Eric. Honestly, I don't think that one is for me.

Mellie is an animation major, so I spoke to her right away. I asked what she likes about it and what kinds of classes her major entails.

"Well," she said, "it's a lot of drawing classes, for sure, but also a lot of computer work."

"I see," I said, nodding. "What would you say has been your favorite class so far?" "Definitely 3D Modeling!" she said excitedly. "I love creating characters."

Her major sounds so fun! I thanked Mellie for her time and started hunting for artists with other majors.

I found a studio art major, a guy named Wade, and he filled me in on what that major requires.
Wade explained that he spends a lot of time in the art studios, creating paintings and pottery.

I've decided that isn't for me either. I'm more of a pen-and-paper artist.

Next up was Abby, who is a graphic design major. She told me about the classes she's been taking and explained that graphic design involves aesthetics.

I'll put that one in my back pocket. I don't mind working on visual layouts at all!

Last, I had to find someone in illustration. I finally cornered a shy girl named Chloe. She wants to illustrate graphic novels. I thought that was pretty cool! All of these majors sound awesome. If I had to pick my favorite, though, it would be between a tie between graphic design and illustration.

I'll think over those two options. In the meantime, though, I guess all I can do is keep drawing!

Saturday, September 23

I slept in today and woke up with the worst bed head ever!

My hair is very curly, and I often don't do too much with it. It's so unruly and unmanageable that only a razor can tame it.

Unfortunately, I forgot to ask Mom to give me a haircut before I left home for school. Now it has grown out and is even messier than usual.

I've only ever had Mom cut my hair, but I'm desperate!

It looks like I'm gonna have to bite the bullet and splurge and get a haircut at an actual salon.

How much will a haircut cost? Lemme do a quick Google search ...

Oof! *That much?* Oh, well. I kind of have no choice.

(Four Hours Later)

I ended up going to one of those "men-only" sporty haircut places. It was okay. I got to watch baseball as they trimmed my mane.

And when they were done ...

Much better!

Of course, they gelled it and everything, so it looks *way* better than it'll ever look again. Tomorrow it should be back to its normal, messy self.

But hey, I'll enjoy this look as long as it lasts. It was so worth the forty bucks!

Sunday, September 24

Max and I went to church together again today. Then, of course, we got milkshakes before going back to the dorms.

I had zero homework, so I took a nap, and I had the strangest dream! Apparently, I'm more worried about school than I thought.
In it, I was all grown-up and was working as an artist.

But I couldn't seem to draw anything good or paint anything better-looking than a kindergartner's finger painting.

Meanwhile, Dani and Nikki were making millions—Dani as a pro soccer player and Nikki as a scientist and musician.

Just after I realized that I was living in a cardboard box, I woke up.

Jolting out of bed, I hurried to the sink and splashed water on my face.

After three big, deep breaths, I felt better. But obviously, I still had some issues to work through.
I decided to take a walk to clear my head.

So what is my deal? Why is it so difficult for me to accept that I'm an artist? Everyone else seems fine with it. In fact, they are encouraging me to take this step.

So the real problem lies within *me*.

Based on my dream, I would think my main concern is money. But that's not it. Sure, I want to make a decent living, but I'd be willing to work at a fast-food joint for the rest of my life if it meant chasing my dreams.

Well, the issue could be success. I've excelled at school my whole life, so going into the unknown world of art is scary. Artists don't care so much about academic standing as they do about talent. But as prideful as I can be at times, I don't think that's the problem either.

No, I know what it is. It's the fear that I'll let people down, that I won't live up to my potential, which is a pointless worry—'cause what if I *am* cut out to be an artist? That means that I'd be wasting my abilities anyway if I didn't at least try.

With new determination, I headed back to my room. I plopped myself down at my desk and began drawing furiously.

Monday, September 25

Guess who stopped by today?

Luis! He brought his newspaper to show me:

It was really impressive! Luis is a very good writer. I especially enjoyed reading his interviews.

He said that everyone in his class got a kick out of my comics.

"I'm glad," I said. "I had fun making them!"

"I could tell," he replied.

A light bulb went off in my head.

Cartooning! That's what I want to do!

It makes me happy when my drawings make others smile. What better way to do that than publishing comic strips?

I wanted to rush to the registrar's office.

But I refrained. I don't want to be too impulsive. I'll take the night to think it over.

In the meantime, I need to catch up on my reading. I haven't finished *The Giver* yet because I've been so busy lately. I hate falling behind with my reading schedule.

(Besides, books oftentimes have lessons in them that have real-world implications. I learn a lot—even from fantasy novels!)

Tuesday, September 26

I've decided that I'm going home this weekend. I'll surprise my family by taking the bus and walking home. (It will take me a good thirty to forty-five minutes, but I'm willing!)

Dani has a soccer match, and I don't want to miss it! Plus, it'll be a good opportunity for me to talk with my parents about my academic plans.

I have Art Club on Friday night, and I have to usher, so I'll leave Saturday morning. Hopefully, Mom or Dad can drive me back to school on Sunday night. If not, I'm cool with taking the bus again.

As comfortable as I've gotten with school, I'm still homesick. I mean, you can't spend your whole life in one place and then just leave it without experiencing *some* emotion.

I'm tired. I want to see my family.

I just wanna go home...

I could tell Max was feeling the same way. He said he's gonna go home this weekend too.

He's been studying really hard lately. He also has been up pretty late every night, working on some project of his. I suspect that he's writing a book.

I'm so proud of how hard he's working.
We both deserve a break!

Wednesday, September 27

If you want to survive in college, *never, ever* forget your room key. Ever.

I was running back to my dorm to grab a book for my next class (yet another thing I forgot) when I realized I didn't have my key on me.

I stood at my door for the longest time, wondering what to do. I was on the verge of panicking because Max was off-campus today, and my RA was in class, so there was no one to let me in.

Suddenly, someone came up behind me. "'Sup, compadre?"

Luis! I frantically explained the situation.
Luis nodded in understanding. "Yo, don't tell anyone I can do this, but ..." Luis stepped up to my door.

I watched in amazement as he proceeded to *pick the lock!*

"How do you know how to do that?" I asked, shocked.

Luis blushed. "I used to accidentally lock myself out of the house all the time. So I learned this neat trick." He smoothly popped the door open.

"Thanks!" I exclaimed.

I rushed into my room, grabbed my book (and my key!), and dashed off to class, shouting another "Thanks!" to Luis over my shoulder.

I swear, that guy is like my guardian angel or something!

Thursday, September 28

As this month draws to a close, I find it amazing that I actually survived!

When I began college, I was determined to make it through, but I had my doubts. Since it's only been about a month, I know I have a long way to go. But still!

I wouldn't say I'm "thriving," but I'm not just merely surviving either.

When I first applied to this school over the summer, I was seriously considering taking a gap year (or a couple, considering how young I am).

My parents convinced me to just jump right in. They said that I'd probably do better if I went to college right away 'cause my knowledge from high school would be fresh in my brain.

That was a good point. What I'd add to that, though, is that the longer you wait, the more daunting college seems.

At least that's how it feels to me.

I also felt pressured to go to school right away because I'm considered a "genius." People were expecting big things from me when all I wanted to do was blend in.

Ha! Fat chance!

Friday, September 29

I was able to go home tonight after all!

Delaney and I were talking at Art Club, and I mentioned that I was heading home this weekend. She said that she was going to her house as well.
I asked her where she lived, and it turns out she's from a town that's only thirty minutes from mine!

Delaney offered to drive me home, since it was on her way. I told her that I wouldn't be done ushering until around ten, but then I got an email *right then* saying that the concert was canceled. (Apparently, the lights went out in the performance hall. Go figure!)

I don't like to feel happy when something works out for me at another's expense, but I couldn't help being relieved!

So after Art Club, I ran back to my dorm—no, really, I was *sprinting*—and packed.
Delaney pulled up five minutes later in her yellow punch-buggy, and we were on
our way!

"I'm so happy you could come with me!" Delaney said as she pulled out of campus.
"I really hate driving alone."
"Me too," I joked, "'cause it'd be illegal."
Delaney laughed.

We had been on the road for a while when Delaney pulled into a gas station.
She filled the tank and went inside the store to pay for it. While she was gone,
I slipped a ten-dollar bill into her cupholder. She seems like the type of person
who would refuse gas money.

When she came back out, she was carrying a box of donuts.
"Here," she said, offering one to me.
"Thanks!" I exclaimed. I was starving!

"So," she said, "Max told me you're gonna join the art department."

I blushed. "Um, yeah. I think I'm going to try an illustration major. Then I could become a cartoonist."
"How fun!" she said. "I'm glad you found something."

"Me too," I replied. "I've been giving it a lot of thought. I brought the paperwork with me to look over this weekend. I'm going to have my parents take a look too."
"It's always nice to get support from loved ones," Delaney said, nodding. She looked a little sad when she said that.

I wonder if maybe some members of her family aren't as supportive of her endeavors. I guess I'm really lucky to have the family that I do.

For the rest of the trip, we talked about movies, favorite video games, and our plans for the (sadly) short weekend.
I gave Delaney directions to my house, and she dropped me off.

"Thanks again!" I called out as she pulled away. "Have a nice weekend!"
"You too!" she said. "I'll pick you up on Sunday."

I walked up to the front door. The lights were all off in my house. Everyone must have gone to bed already.

Luckily, I have a house key on my keyring, so I quietly unlocked the door, stepped into the house, and closed and relocked the door behind me.

It had been a while since I'd been home, and I hadn't realized how good it would feel to be back!
I quickly climbed the stairs to my bedroom and put my stuff down.
I was struggling to decide whether or not to wake my family up. I flopped down on my bed, thinking.

Nah, I'll let them be. I want to surprise them in the morning!

Saturday, September 30

When I woke up in the morning, I looked at the clock, and it was 10:00 a.m.!

I quickly got up and changed clothes. I heard voices coming from downstairs, so I knew my family was eating breakfast in the kitchen. I casually trotted down the stairs, grabbed some cereal, and sat next to them at the table. The looks on their faces were priceless!

"Graham!" they collectively yelled.
I was bowled over with a group hug.

Of course, I had to explain to my parents *how* I had gotten got home and why I hadn't sent them a text to let them know I was coming.

Danielle was especially psyched to see me. "You're coming to my game, right?" she asked.

"Of course!" I said.

She squealed (very unlike her) and slugged my shoulder (very much like her).

It was a fantastic day of eating home-cooked meals, catching up on what I'd missed at home, and telling my family about my college experience.

I talked about my friends and described Art Club. Dad and I watched some baseball games he had recorded. Mom quickly did some laundry for me (I had stuffed as many articles of clothing into my duffel bag as I could). Nikki chased me around the house, insisting that she and Marie needed to serenade me with her saxophone. And Dani talked me to death about the latest episode of *The Mandalorian*.

I've really, really missed everyone! They missed me too, apparently. When Josh came in from his doghouse, he nearly smothered me with doggy kisses!

I really missed him too!

The day went by way too fast. Before I knew it, it was 5:00 p.m., and we had to take Dani to the soccer match. Dad let me drive, and surprisingly, we made it there in one piece. Dani ran off to join her team while the rest of us found seats on the bleachers.

The opponents Dani's team were up against were their biggest rival. They were formidable, with no losses (yet). Dani had been super nervous during the car ride, but I also saw a determination within her.

The ref blew the whistle, and the game began!

Dani was great! I could tell she'd been practicing. Her team squeaked by with a 3-2 win over their rivals.

Dani, naturally, scored the winning goal.

She ran up to us after the game, sweaty and panting but smiling.

"Way to go, sis!" I said. "You were awesome out there!"
"Thanks," she said as we walked to the car. "I played extra hard 'cause you were here, Graham."

Dad announced that we would be going for celebratory ice cream. A cheer erupted from the van.

We got to the ice cream parlor, ordered our regulars, and sat down in a booth.

I lifted my dish in a salute. "For Dani," I said, "because you've worked so hard. You really came through for your team."
She blushed, then raised her dish. "To Mom and Dad, for helping all of us kids chase our dreams!"

Dad lifted his dish (which still had a lot of ice cream in it). "To Nikki, for trying new things. We're really proud of you, sweetie."

Mom raised her cup (she had a root beer float). "And to Graham, for making it through what I'm sure was a tough first month of school. Not only are you doing very well, but you've found out what you want your major to be! Way to go, honey!"

Nikki raised her kiddie dish. "To our family!" she cried.

We all laughed. "To family," I concluded.
We knocked our dishes together.

(Yes, I know how cheesy we are.)

We all finished up our treats, then got back in the car to head home. The rest of the night was filled with board games and conversation. With time to relax and have fun, I was able to reflect on all I've learned.

Smiling and laughing with my family, I realized that I am truly blessed. Come what may, I have hope for my future. Even if I go through hard times, I'll keep a smile on my face.

And when it feels like my world is crumbling, my friends and family will help me pick up the pieces.

Honestly, I'm excited to continue my journey.

I can't wait to see what comes next!

About the Author

M. D. Nowak is an animator and illustrator who loves every aspect of storytelling. She is experienced at creating webcomics that includes her work, *Airball.* *Composition: Graham* is her first book.

Printed in the United States
by Baker & Taylor Publisher Services